First U.S. paperback edition 2010

The Library of Congress has cataloged
the hardcover edition as follows:

Dunbar, Polly.
Penguin / Polly Dunbar. —1st U.S. ed.
p.   cm.
Summary: Ben is delighted to receive a penguin for
his birthday but Penguin will not answer or respond
to him in any way, no matter what Ben does, until,
at last, they discover the language of friendship.
ISBN 978-0-7636-3404-9 (hardcover)
[1. Penguins—Fiction.
2. Human-animal communication—Fiction.
3. Friendship—Fiction.]   I. Title.
PZ7.D89445 Pen 2007
[E]—dc22   2007024190

ISBN 978-0-7636-4972-2 (paperback)

12 13 14 15 16 SWT 10 9 8 7 6 5 4 3 2

Printed in Dongguan, Guangdong, China

This book was typeset in Windsor.
The illustrations were done in mixed media.

Candlewick Press
99 Dover Street
Somerville, Massachusetts 02144

visit us at www.candlewick.com

Penguin

Polly Dunbar

CANDLEWICK PRESS

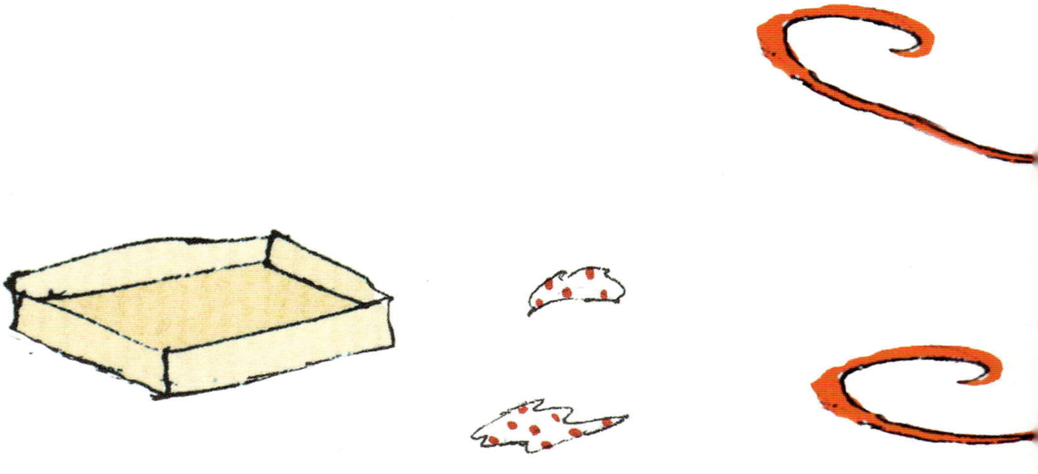

Ben ripped open his present.

Inside was a penguin.

"Hello, Penguin!" said Ben.

"What shall we play?" said Ben.

Penguin said nothing.

"Can't you talk?" said Ben.

Penguin said nothing.

Ben tickled Penguin.

Penguin didn't laugh.

Ben made his funniest face
for Penguin.

Penguin didn't laugh.

Ben put on a happy hat

and sang a silly song

and did a dizzy dance.

Penguin said nothing.

"Will you talk to me if I stand on
my head?" said Ben.

Penguin didn't say a word.

So Ben prodded Penguin

and stuck out his tongue at Penguin.

Penguin said nothing.

Ben made fun of Penguin

and imitated Penguin.

Penguin said nothing.

Ben ignored Penguin.

Penguin ignored Ben.

So Ben fired **Penguin** into outer space.

Penguin came back to Earth without a word.

Ben tried to feed Penguin
to a passing lion.

Penguin said nothing.

Lion didn't want to eat Penguin.

Ben got upset.

Penguin said nothing.

Lion ate Ben

for being too noisy.

Penguin bit Lion
very hard
on the nose.

said Lion.

said Ben.

And Penguin said . . .

everything!

Polly Dunbar, a recipient of a *Publishers Weekly* Cuffie Award for Most Promising New Illustrator, is the author-illustrator of *Dog Blue* and the illustrator of *Here's a Little Poem: A Very First Book of Poetry*. Of the inspiration for *Penguin*, she says, "I wrote this story for my brother Ben. He gave me the original Penguin, who is very old and made of black velvet. He said, 'You can have Penguin, if you look after him . . . but be careful: he bites!' This gave me the idea for the story." When not creating children's books, Polly Dunbar works as a freelance illustrator. She lives in Brighton, England.